The Cross-Eyed Rabbit

The Cross-Eyed Rabbit

written and illustrated by
Claude Boujon

Margaret K. McElderry Books
NEW YORK

Published originally under the title *Le lapin loucheur*
Copyright © 1984 by l'école des loisirs, Paris
English translation copyright © 1988 by Margaret K. McElderry Books,
Macmillan Publishing Company

Margaret K. McElderry Books
Macmillan Publishing Company
866 Third Avenue
New York, NY 10022

Composition by Linoprint Composition Co., Inc.
New York, New York
Printed by General Offset Co., Inc.
Jersey City, New Jersey
Bound by The Book Press
Brattleboro, Vermont

First American Edition

Printed in the United States of America

10   9   8   7   6   5   4   3   2   1

Library of Congress Cataloging-in-Publication Data

Boujon, Claude.
The cross-eyed rabbit.

Translation of: Le lapin loucheur.
Summary: A visually-impaired rabbit comes to the
aid of his two brothers when a fox threatens their
lives.
[1. Rabbits—Fiction.   2. Visually handicapped—
Fiction.   3. Physically handicapped—Fiction]   I. Title.
PZ7.B6627Cr   1988   [E]   87-22847
ISBN 0-689-50443-8

The Cross-Eyed Rabbit

Three rabbits, who were brothers, lived in a clearing in the woods where they had dug a comfortable burrow. Two of the brothers were always together, but the third was often alone.

He was cross-eyed and his brothers couldn't help laughing at him. They kept chanting, "Look to the right to see to the left. Look up to see down. Ah-ha-ha, ah-ha-ha!"

His brothers' teasing troubled the poor cross-eyed rabbit a lot, but he didn't complain.

Like all rabbits, the three brothers loved to look at the full moon. But when the cross-eyed rabbit exclaimed, "How beautiful the two moons are!" the others, who saw only one moon, called him a liar. It was very unfair because the cross-eyed rabbit really saw two moons, one with each of his eyes.

To escape from his brothers' unkindness, the cross-eyed rabbit would take refuge in the burrow and make up poems.

Since he could not write in a straight line and looked at what he had written crookedly, he wrote a single poem in many ways.

"I love cabbage like crazy," was followed by: "How I love crazy cabbage," or "I love a crazy like cabbage." He found this great fun.

On the subject of cabbage, at least, his brothers admired him. He had an amazing appetite. In spite of his crooked eyes, he could go straight to the biggest cabbage and chew it up completely.

But one night, when the moon was behind a cloud, a fox came to the woods. He loved to eat rabbits and he smelled a delicious meal not far away.

Certain that he would be feasting soon, he went along without hurrying and sang gaily, "To satisfy hunger, one rabbit is not enough. It is much better to eat two, and three are a feast fit for a king!"

His nose had not deceived him. He reached the clearing and saw, without being seen, the cross-eyed rabbit's brothers.

The fox stopped, his nose close to the ground, but a blade of grass tickled his nose and he sneezed, "Ah-ah-t-chou-oum!"

The two rabbits caught a glimpse of him—and ran away as fast as they could go.

They had a good start on the fox and felt
certain they'd escape him without any
trouble. They climbed up hills and rushed
down them, sometimes capering carelessly
on mossy spots. And, keeping hidden in the
undergrowth, they called out, "Coucou."

Little by little, dawn drove away the darkness and the fox gained on them.

Now the two foolish rabbits felt the fox's breath on their backs.

"Each for himself!" one of the brothers cried. "We'll take refuge in our burrow."

They changed their direction suddenly to get back to the clearing.

All the while, the cross-eyed rabbit was sleeping peacefully in the burrow. He was dreaming. He dreamed of an enormous carrot, a carrot that could only exist in a rabbit's dream.

He recited a poem to it.

> Carrot,
> Orange-red,
> while my brothers
> who have itchy feet
> run through the woods,
> with my teeth
> I will crunch you.

Just outside, close to the sleeping rabbit, the situation was very serious. The fox had reached the burrow first and, with the tip of his bushy tail, he was blocking the entrance.

Paralyzed with fright, the two rabbits believed their last hour had come.

Just then, the
cross-eyed rabbit woke up and,
without suspecting anything,
put his nose out of the burrow.
And there—oh what a miracle!
He saw the tip of a carrot
exactly like the huge one
in his dream!

Without looking
any closer, he bit hard
with all his teeth
right into this
appetizing treat,
which was—

the fox's tail.

The fox ran away howling. The cross-eyed rabbit's two brothers were saved.

"Thank you!" they said to him. "Without you, that dreadful beast would have eaten us. Your vision is still peculiar, but we do admire your bite."

Now, the three rabbits are together all the time. When the cross-eyed rabbit sees two moons, his brothers are sorry they only see one.